A GIRAFFE
Goes to Paris

by Mary Tavener Holmes & John Harris

illustrated by Jon Cannell

MARSHALL CAVENDISH CHILDREN

ACKNOWLEDGMENTS

The authors would like to thank the following for giving permission to reproduce the historic artifacts and artwork in this book:

Nicolas Huet, "Study of the Giraffe," given to Charles X by the viceroy of Egypt, watercolor, New York, the Morgan Library and Museum.

Cavalcade à la Giraffe, souvenir and possible entry ticket, etching, E. C. Couplet, 1827, Waddesdon, the Rothschild Collection (the National Trust); photographer: University of Central England Digital Services.

Colored image of the rotunda, Gabriel Thouin, Plans Raisonnées de Toutes les Espèces de Jardins, 1820, hand-colored lithograph, plate 37: Jardin du Roi, the Metropolitan Museum of Art, Harris Brisbane Dick Fund, 1935 (35.20).

The black-and-white map, M. Boitard, Le Jardin des Plantes. Descriptions et Moeurs des Mammiferes, 1842, map of *Le Jardin des Plantes* by Paul Legrand, etching and aquatint, the Metropolitan Museum of Art, Gift of Lincoln Kirstein, 1979 (1979.600.1).

Fer à repasser orné d'un motif giraffe. (IRON)
Billet d'entré pour voir la giraffe. (ENTRY TICKET)
Plat à barbe décor á la giraffe. (BARBER BOWL)
from the collection of Muséum Nationale d'Histoire Naturelle, 38, rue Geoffroy Saint-Hilaire, Paris, France

François Gérard, Charles X (detail), Versailles, Musée National du Château (Réunion des Musées Nationaux/Art Resource NY).

La Girafe by Antoine Louis Barye, Paris, Musée du Louvre (RF 238).

Text copyright © 2010 by Mary Tavener Holmes and John Harris
Illustrations copyright © 2010 by Jon Cannell
All rights reserved
Marshall Cavendish Corporation, 99 White Plains Road, Tarrytown, NY 10591
www.marshallcavendish.us/kids

Library of Congress Cataloging-in-Publication Data
Holmes, Mary Tavener.
A giraffe goes to Paris / by Mary Tavener Holmes and John Harris ;
illustrated by Jon Cannell. — 1st ed.
    p. cm.
Summary: Recounts the 1827 journey of a young giraffe named Belle, who was given by the Pasha of Egypt to the King of France, as she made her way by boat and land to Paris, accompanied by her devoted caretaker, Atir.
ISBN 978-0-7614-5595-0
[1. Voyages and travels—Fiction. 2. Giraffe—Fiction. 3. Animal
introduction—Fiction. 4. France—History—19th century—Fiction.] I.
Harris, John, 1950 July 7– II. Cannell, Jon, ill. III. Title.
PZ7.H7373Gir 2010
[E]—dc22
2009019047

The illustrations are rendered in watercolor and ink.
Book design by Jon Cannell
Art Director: Anahid Hamparian
Editor: Margery Cuyler
Printed in Malaysia (T)
First edition
1 3 5 6 4 2

 Marshall Cavendish Children

Shhhhhhh.
Look.
The moon.
The moon over Paris!

And there...in the moonlight...
what is that?
A giraffe.
My giraffe.
Belle.

BELLE

born 1824

The French people called her the *belle enfant des tropiques*—
"the beautiful child from the tropics." Which she was. And is.

MUHAMMAD ALI
Pasha of Egypt
1769–1849

CHARLES X
King of France
1757–1836

She was a present from the great pasha of Egypt, Muhammad Ali, to the king of France, Charles X. No one in France had ever seen a giraffe. No one. So she was the perfect present.

ME!
Atir

I was chosen to take care of Belle on her long, long journey from Egypt. My name, I should tell you, is Atir.

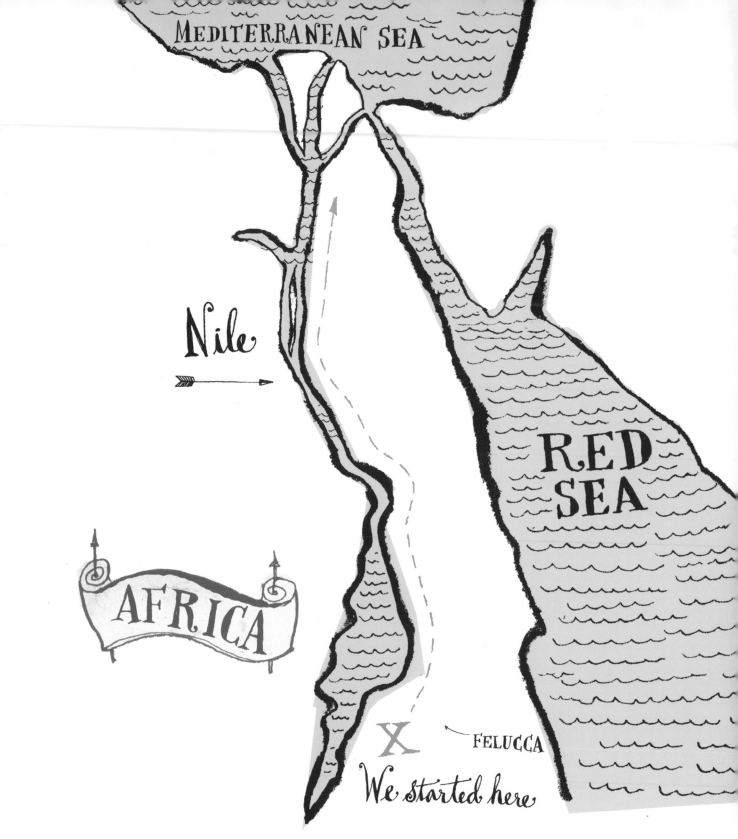

First we went on a boat trip on the ancient River Nile—

Belle and I and men from the pasha's court.

And what, you may ask, does a giraffe eat while floating down the River Nile? Giraffes, after all, nibble on treetops. But where would Belle find treetops in the middle of a mighty river?

And what would she eat on the even longer trip to France?

COW Nº1

COW Nº2

COW Nº3

We thought and thought . . . and decided she should drink milk.
Milk was the best idea. But a young giraffe (Belle was only two)
drinks a lot of milk—which is why we brought three cows with us.
And, to keep Belle company, two antelopes.

ANTELOPE Nº1

ANTELOPE Nº2

Once we got Belle onboard the ship, we saw right away that there was another problem. A big problem. Belle wasn't going to fit! It was too dangerous to keep her above on the deck, and she was too tall to sail in the cramped quarters below.

It was then that our Italian captain came up with a brilliant idea. He cut a hole in the deck, so Belle's long, graceful neck could poke out. He lined the hole with straw to protect her from the rough, splintery edges. He provided an umbrella to protect her from the sun and rain.

And off we went. Our destination: France.

I DUE FRATELLI

When Belle walked calmly down the gangplank, the people of Marseille could not believe their eyes. Never in their lives had they seen such a creature! She was twelve feet tall and—what was she, exactly? They could not decide. Was she some kind of camel? She had spots like a leopard's. She had a long tongue, almost like a snake's. And she walked so strangely— first her two right legs, then her two left legs—so she was not a horse. What was she? Everyone had a different idea.

Fancy Parties!

Belle and I stayed in the private home of a rich lady, a countess, who threw lavish parties in Belle's honor. The parties were fun.

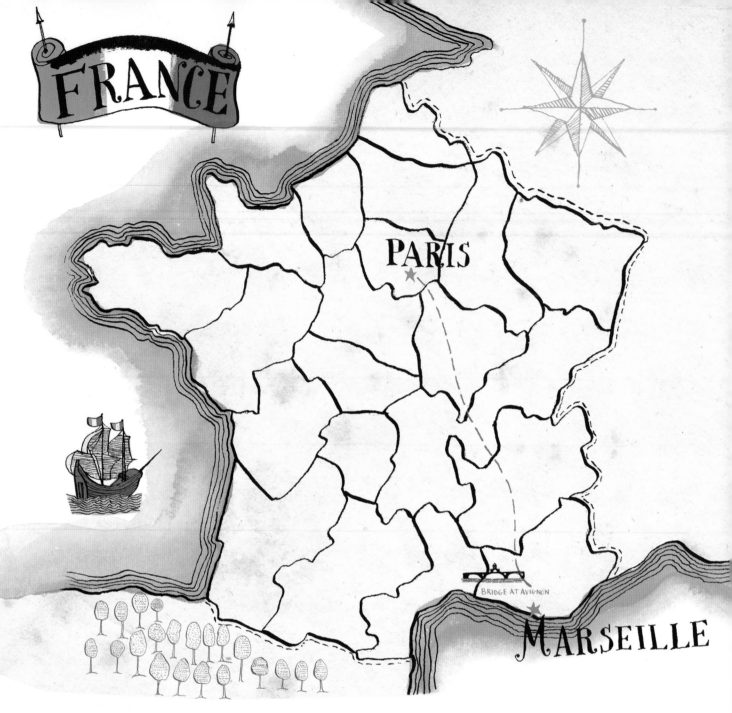

FRANCE

PARIS

BRIDGE AT AVIGNON

MARSEILLE

But remember . . . we had to get to Paris to the king, who was awaiting Belle's arrival five hundred miles away.

How?

We were all tired of boat trips. Belle was, too, and no cart was big enough to hold her.

Belle seemed to be enjoying her strolls around the city of Marseille.

Why not WALK to Paris?

And so that's what we did.

But we would need help—someone to lead such a complicated operation. Who?

We thought and thought, until the rich lady said, "Geoffroy Saint-Hilaire. He's the great professor at the Museum of Natural History in Paris. He's a friend of mine, and *he* could do it."

Professor Saint-Hilaire took charge immediately and devised a plan. Over a period of eight weeks, we would walk with Belle the entire way from Marseille to Paris.

8 WEEKS

Marseille → Paris

FOOD

HORNS ARE KNOBS OF CARTILAGE

EVERY GIRAFFE HAS DIFFERENT SPOTS, LIKE FINGERPRINTS

18"

GIRAFFE TONGUE

ÉTIENNE GEOFFROY SAINT-HILAIRE

1772–1844

Species GIRAFFA CAMELOPARDALIS

Belle-wear

fig. No 1

But Belle, like any traveler setting out on a long journey, would need to have the right clothes. She had arrived in France without so much as a raincoat. And a raincoat, in fact, was precisely what she needed to protect her from the rain, the sun, and the wind.

France is not Egypt! And we did not want her catching a cold in her long, long throat. We came up with a waterproof outfit—a blanket that buttoned around her body, embroidered on one side with the coat of arms of France and on the other with the coat of arms of the pasha of Egypt. It was edged in heavy black braid. She wore it as a cape around her neck—this looked very good on her—and, I am serious, boots. Yes, boots. She was not used to walking such long distances.

To keep Belle-wear tidy, you need a Belle-iron!

Our Caravan!

We set out: French gendarmes in front, the cows (remember them?), one or two Egyptians in full dress, then the professor (walking alone), Belle in her finery (with me in front holding an umbrella over her head), horses drawing a wagon loaded with supplies, the antelopes (remember the antelopes?), and some sheep.

Crowds lined the roads. People were hanging from the trees to be closer to her when she nibbled on the leaves. I'm not sure what they were expecting—a wild beast? A ferocious creature? Instead, they saw Belle, my Belle, gentle and elegant—the best-dressed animal in the world, and she didn't make a sound.

MADEMOISELLE
BELLE

AUBERGE À LA GIRAFE

We stopped at inns that put out special signs: AUBERGE À LA GIRAFE
Church bells rang as we made our way through the air that smelled of lavender
and lilac and roses. The fields were thick with olive groves, poppies, and grapevines.

ATIR

AVIGNON

The newspapers announced we were coming, and people streamed out to see us. We made our way through cities with magical names: AIX-EN-PROVENCE, the town of a thousand fountains; AVIGNON, the ancient city where the popes once lived; then onward through ORANGE and VALENCE. So many towns saw Belle.

Sur le pont d'Avignon,
l'on y danse, l'on y danse.
Sur le pont d'Avignon,
l'on y danse touse en rond.

PLACE BELLECOURT
JUNE 6, 1827

On June 6, 1827, we arrived in Lyons. Belle walked gracefully under the city gate and into the beautiful Place Bellecourt, where thirty thousand people came to see her in a single day. Oh, it was grand.

ATIR

But Paris was, as always, our destination: Paris and the king.

Paris loves Belle!

Paris began to prepare for Belle's arrival. Paris began to go crazy!

CAVALCADE A LA GIRAFFE.

A souvenir ticket

INK

Barber bowl decorated with beautiful
Belle and her faithful Atir

Belle in bronze by Barye

There were giraffe songs, poems, paintings, pottery, fabrics, cough-drop boxes,
wallpaper, toys, inkwells, jewelry, and gingerbread cookies. There was a giraffe
piano with strings going straight up the neck and a giraffe hairdo with wire
inside. The hairdo was so tall that a wealthy lady wearing it would have to sit
on the floor of her carriage to fit inside.

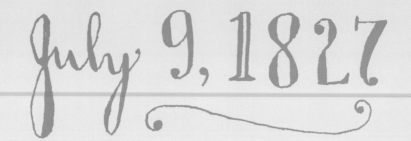

July 9, 1827

On July 9, 1827, the great moment finally arrived. Belle met the king...
and ate rose petals out of his hand.

The king's children petted her beautiful, spotted legs.
The grand duchesse de Berry hung a garland of flowers around Belle's neck.
And as for me . . . the king gave me, Atir, a thousand francs!

Paris
JARDIN des PLANTES

And so began our eighteen years in Paris.

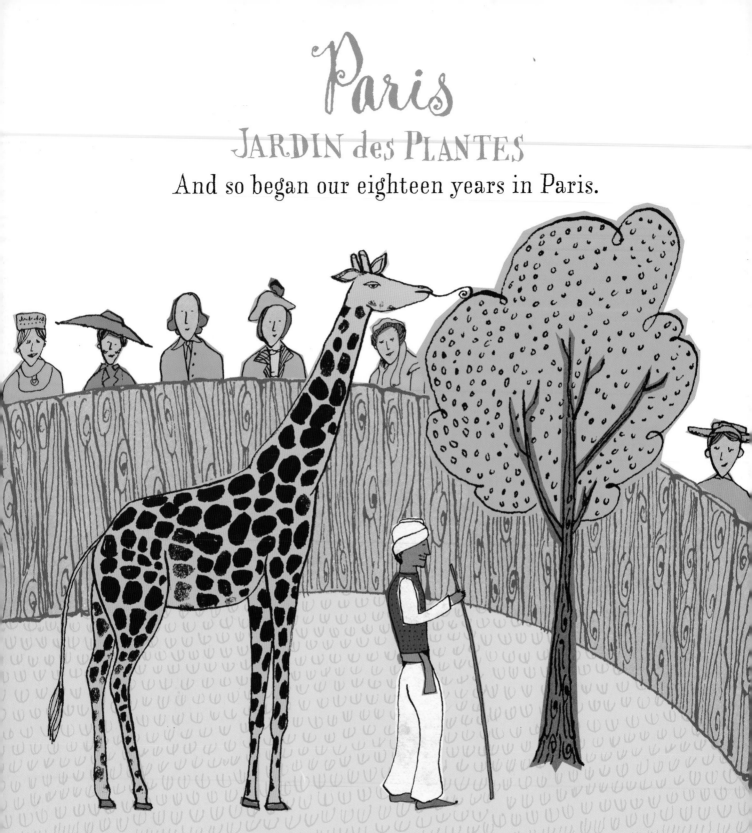

In the first six months, more than six hundred thousand Parisians came to see us—*paid* to see us! Dressed in my best—my white turban, my fancy vest, and my wide Egyptian pants—I would take Belle out on a leisurely two-hour walk through the lovely Jardin des Plantes, where the Parisians had made a home for us in the Rotunda.

The people would watch us, not believing their eyes.

LE JARDIN DES PLANTES.

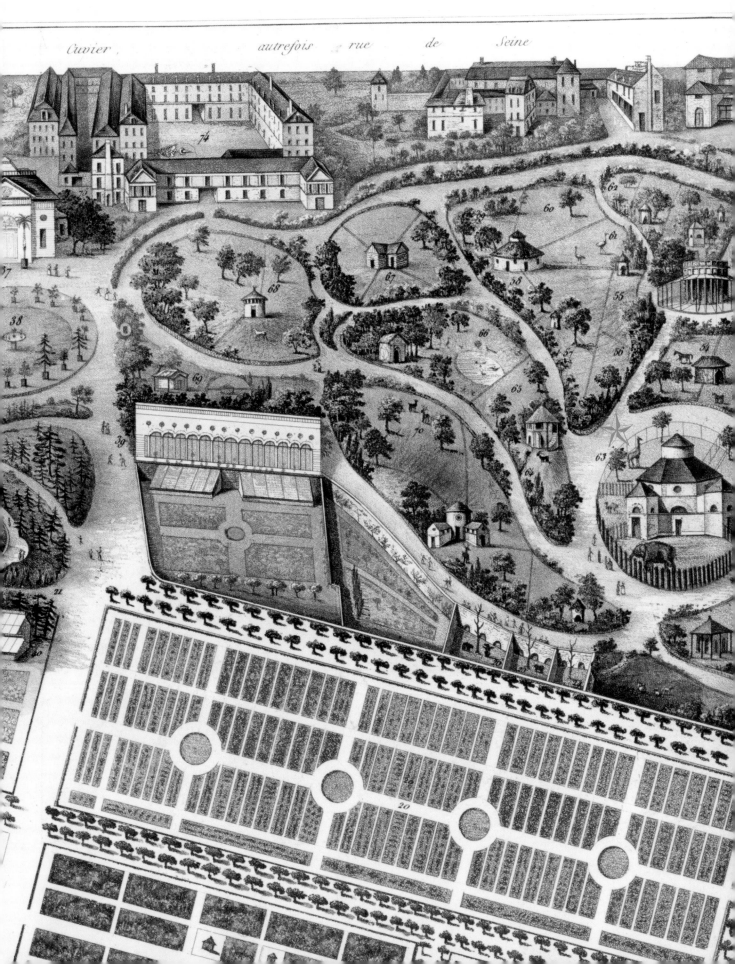

Cuvier, *autrefois rue de Seine*

ROTUNDA

In the Rotunda, I have a small sleeping balcony in Belle's specially heated room. I'm right up near her head, so I can pet her.

Shhhhh. Belle is getting sleepy, and I am, too. But before we both drift off, let's take one last look together at the moon.

Bonne nuit, ma chère Belle.

Belle's journey really happened!

The authors got most of their information from *Une Girafe pour le Roi*, Catalogue de l'Exposition du Musée de l'Ile-de-France, Château de Sceaux, 1984; Gabriel Dardaud, *Une Girafe pour le Roi*, Paris, 1985; and Michael Allin, *Zarafa*, New York, 1999.

Some people refer to our Belle as Zarafa, taking her name from the Arabic—*zurafah* or *zirafah*—a word with many meanings, including "creature of grace" and "tall one." Many scholars believe the word *giraffe* comes originally from that Arabic word.

PRONUNCIATION GUIDE

Auberge à la Girafe—oh-BEARJ ah la gee-RAF

Au rendez-vous de la Girafe—oh ren-day-VOO de la gee-RAF

Avignon—ah-VEEN-yon

Bonne nuit, ma chère Belle—bon WEET, ma share Bell

Des Tropiques—day troh-PEEKS

Duchesse du Berry—do-SHESS do bear-EE

Enfant—on-FON

Geoffroy Saint-Hilaire—jeff-RAY sant-HE-lair

Jardin des Plantes—zhar-DAN day PLONT

Lyons—LEE-on

Marseille—Mar-SAY

Orange—o-RAHNJ

Place Bellecourt—Plass bell-KOOR

Provence—pro-VANZ

Valence—VAH-lonz

Ticket to see her!